For Oliver

First Edition

Published in Great Britain by ABC, All Books for Children,
a division of the All Children's Company Ltd.,
33 Museum Street, London WC1A 1LD, England

ISBN 0-316-61201-4

Library of Congress Cataloging-in-Publication information is available.

10 9 8 7 6 5 4 3 2 1

Published simultaneously in Canada
by Little, Brown & Company (Canada) Limited

Printed in Hong Kong

A
Mammoth
Imagination

Philip Ross Norman

Little, Brown and Company
Boston Toronto London

The Wild Boars were having
a huge feast.

"Eat, eat, eat," little Bonbon
said with a sniff. "That's all they
ever do. I wish someone would
play with me."

Bonbon was bored. But the
grown-ups just kept on eating
until it was time to go to sleep.

The next day was no better. There was nothing left to eat after the feast, so now the Wild Boars had to look for some more food.

"Come on, Bonbon," urged Burper. "Hurry up!"

But Bonbon wasn't interested in food. He was busy being a monster, scaring away wild animals. "Oh, Bonbon! One day your imagination will get you into trouble," sighed Muncher. But Bonbon didn't care. He was a monster. "*Rooarrhh!*" he yelled. Suddenly, he heard leaves rustling and twigs snapping.

"What was that?" he wondered. Bonbon stopped playing and hurried to catch up with the grown-ups. Looking over his shoulder, Bonbon thought he could see something big and furry moving in the mist.

The Wild Boars stopped
at a cave to pick mushrooms.
"It's perfect for hide-and-seek!"
Bonbon said. "There are so many
tunnels — you'll never find me!"
He wandered around. There
were paintings of furry animals
all over the walls. "Monsters!"
he squeaked. "Like the ones
in the forest!"
"Don't be silly," said Burper.
"They're mammoths."
"And there are no
mammoths anymore," added
Dribbles. "They're extinct."
"But I saw them!" said Bonbon.

"Don't be silly," said
Burper. "It's just your imagination
again. Now, help us with these mushrooms."

After their meal,
the grown-ups rested and
Bonbon played quietly by
himself. When he looked up,
he saw that it had begun to
snow. "I'm going to make a
snowboar!" he yelped.

When it was almost finished,

he ran to get the grown-ups.

"Come and look at my
snowboar!" he cried.

"In a minute," said Burper.

Bonbon waited and waited. A
minute seemed to take a very long time.

"Oh well, I'll finish it by myself,"
Bonbon sighed, and he ran back to
the snowboar.

Bonbon stared at it. It looked
different. He looked more closely.
The snowboar had eyes and a nose!

Someone had finished it for him.

All around the snowboar were
big footprints, bigger even than
the grown-ups'.

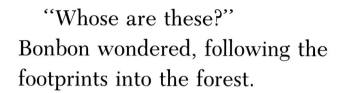

"Whose are these?"
Bonbon wondered, following the
footprints into the forest.

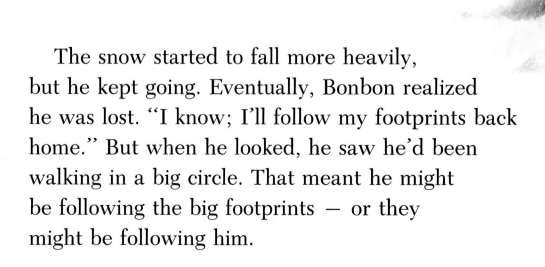

The snow started to fall more heavily,
but he kept going. Eventually, Bonbon realized
he was lost. "I know; I'll follow my footprints back
home." But when he looked, he saw he'd been
walking in a big circle. That meant he might
be following the big footprints — or they
might be following him.

Bonbon was very
scared. He looked
around, trembling.

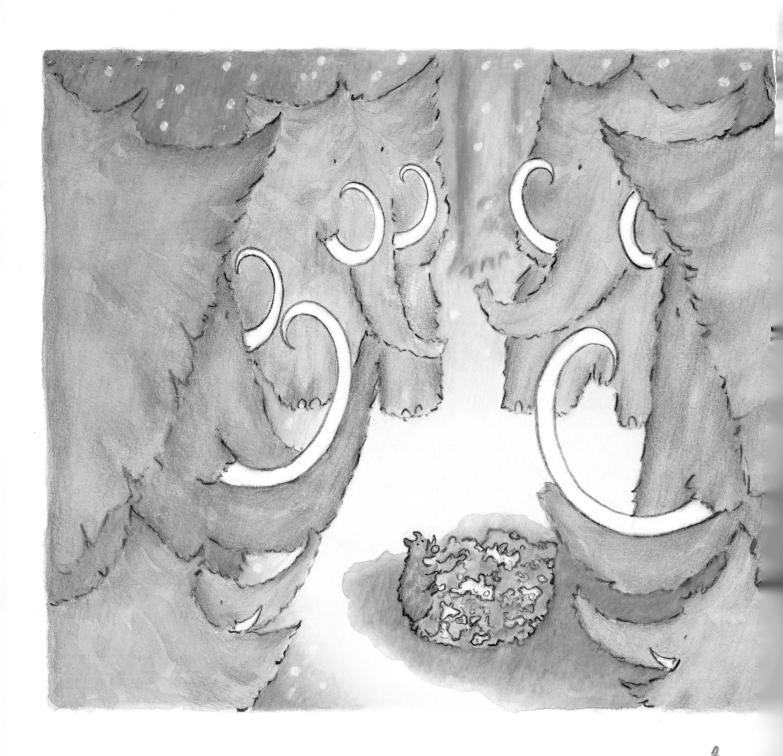

Mammoths!

Huge, furry mammoths, much
bigger than in the cave paintings,
were all around him!

"Oh," squealed Bonbon, jumping
up and down. To his surprise, the
mammoths turned and ran away.
  They were
frightened of him!

"Wait — don't leave me
here! I'm lost!" squeaked Bonbon.
  The mammoths stopped and
whispered to one another. Then
one of them lifted Bonbon
gently onto her back with
her furry trunk.

With a slow plod,

plod of giant feet,

the mammoths

threaded their

way through the

sparkling trees.

Bonbon wasn't scared
anymore. "Just wait until
I tell the others!" he thought.

The mammoths took Bonbon home to their cave. The baby mammoths led Bonbon inside to see their toys and their paintings.

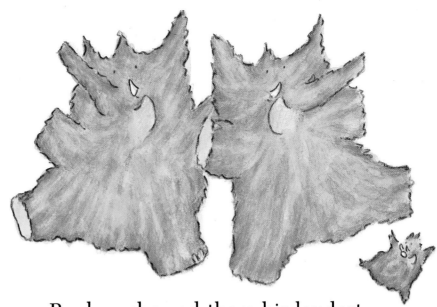

Bonbon showed them his loudest roar. They taught him to swim in their hot pool. And their beds were much better for jumping than his! When they finally stopped, they could hear music from outside.

Bonbon had never
heard such a beautiful
sound before. While some
of the mammoths lifted up
their trunks and sang a woolly
mammoth song, others did a
slow woolly mammoth dance.

Soon the baby mammoths were
sleepy. The big mammoths carried
them inside and tucked them into bed.

While the little mammoths slept, Bonbon listened
to the big mammoths tell stories of long ago.

Soon it was time for Bonbon to
go home. The mammoths showed him
which way to go and waved good-bye.
    Bonbon hurried. He knew the grown-up
boars would be worrying about him.

In his rush, he tripped and fell into a
berry patch, but he didn't even stop to eat.

At last, he was home.

"Where have you been?" asked Burper.

Bonbon opened his mouth to tell them, and then stopped. They wouldn't believe him. They'd say it was just his imagination. "I've been picking berries," he said.

"So you have," said Muncher, pulling them out of Bonbon's fur.

Dribbles made a juicy berry cake,
and Bonbon was so hungry, he ate it all.

The next day, when the grown-ups were
resting after lunch, Bonbon skipped off.

"Don't you want us to play with you?"
asked Burper.

"Would you like a basket to collect
more berries?"asked Muncher.

"No, thanks," called Bonbon. "I'll have
more fun with my mammoth imagination!"